JAMIE'S GIFT

A YOUNG TEEN'S GUIDE TO FEARS, WORRIES,
AND OTHER LIFE CHALLENGES
(LIKE BEING IRRITATED BY OTHER PEOPLE)

by brinsley hammond-brouwer
and jenifer trivelli, m.s.

PUBLISHER'S NOTE: This is a work of fiction. The authors represent scientific and theoretical constructs to the best of their knowledge, and provide references in text when available. Names, characters, and situations are from our own lived experiences or our imaginations, and any resemblance to actual persons is coincidental.

Jamie's Gift: a young teen's guide to fears, worries, and other life challenges (like being irritated by other people) / Brinsley Hammond-Brouwer & Jenifer Trivelli, M.S.

ISBN (paperback) 978-0-6927-8691-8
ISBN (ebook) 978-0-6927-8692-5

YAF058110 YOUNG ADULT FICTION / Social Themes / Emotions & Feelings
YAN051200 YOUNG ADULT NONFICTION / Social Topics / Self-Esteem & Self-Reliance
YAF058060 YOUNG ADULT FICTION / Social Themes / Depression

Jamie's Gift is available at a discount when purchased in quantity. For more information, contact WiseMindEd@yahoo.com

dedicated to everyone who has loved us
through our often challenging processes of
self-discovery, and all adults and children
navigating this journey of self-understanding
together

Authors' Note:

Be sure to pace yourself with the chapters in this book. We did our best to present the material in an entertaining way; yet it is fairly dense material and easier to digest in the chapter chunks laid out. You may be tempted to read the entire book in one sitting, and we promise you that you will get a better result if you go slow.

These strategies are adaptable. The same thing might not work for everyone. You don't have to take the instructions word for word, and don't be afraid to tweak the strategies you are given. If the original concept doesn't quite work, try to reflect: *Why didn't this work for me?* Maybe it's as simple as being in the wrong setting, and moving to a different room will fix the problem. And if that doesn't work, try something else. It doesn't hurt to try.

Contents

jamie's journal

read only with my permission!

INTRODUCTION

I was supposed to be cleaning my room, but instead I was procrastinating, when I found it.

"It" was sitting in a desk drawer that I hadn't opened in a while (five years, to be exact), so the drawer stuck when I tried to open it. But that's not important. What I found *inside* the drawer was important.

It didn't look like much - a pile of yellowing pages covered in text, tied in a bundle with a fraying piece of twine. But I lifted it out of the drawer anyway. And as I untied the twine, I realized what it was.

Wait. I should tell you about myself. My name is Jamie. I'm 13. I'm an artist, or I like to think I am. I have twin crazy younger sisters and extroverted parents who love me but don't understand me. My dark hair covers my eyes most of the time. I like music. My favorite color is green. I have two cats and a dog.

That's pretty much it.

Anyway, so I untied the twine and read the first page. *Comprehensive Manual for Managing Intense Emotional States, by Walter M. Cunningham*, was written in the middle of the first page. And I remembered it.

My grandpa left me this pile of papers, this "manual," when he died. I was eight then, and couldn't even get through the first page of dense, tiny lines of scientific-sounding text. It might be easier now, though - I'm five years older and a lot smarter. I pick up the page -

"Jamie!" I hear from downstairs. "Time for school supply shopping! Come on!"

"Coming!" I call down. But as I open the door I look back at it, curious as to what the pages might say.

CHAPTER 1
my mom asks me about school

"How was the first day of school?" my mom asks at dinner.

I don't know what to say, so I don't say anything. I mean, it was school. What is there to say about it? And why do parents always ask?

"Jamie?"

"WHAT?" I yell. I'm not sure why I snapped. But why does she have to bug me so much? What if I don't want to talk all day, every day like she does? What if I just want to eat my boring dinner of meatloaf and Brussels sprouts in peace?

"What's wrong?"

"Nothing!" I feel like I'm being buried, or suffocated, in a mining tunnel or something and I have to get out now.

Mom looks confused. She knows something is wrong, and so do I. I just don't know what.

"Jamie, something is obviously wrong. What's going on? Maybe I can help..."

She trails off as I put my head in my hands. "I don't KNOW what's going on! Can you just leave me alone?!?"

"I really think that talking about it will -"

Her pressing questions are too much. The walls are closing in on me. My breath starts to get fast as I get more and more agitated. I try to calm down, to take deep breaths, but thinking about my breaths just makes them shallower, and my heart beat faster. I imagine a turtle pulling into its shell. Thoughts ricochet in my brain like speeding bullets. *Mom doesn't understand. Why does she have to ask so many questions? Can't she leave me alone? Why am I so upset? Is something wrong with me? Is it normal to feel like this?*

"Jamie?"

She can't reach me in my protective turtle shell. She doesn't understand. I can't answer her. My brain is about to explode, and she won't stop bugging me for answers to a question I don't even know.

I storm upstairs and slam my bedroom door. Hard. Something falls off my desk. It's Grandpa's manual!

The pages scatter all over the floor, and it takes me forever to organize them. I handle each one delicately, though. I'm determined not to vent my frustration on my grandpa's last gift to me. As far as I know, this is the only copy in existence.

Finally, they're back in order. I look at the first page. *The Basics: Get to Know Your Protector Brain and Your Wise Mind,* I read. I skim the page, then figure that I have nothing better to do (unless you count sulking as better) and read it.

THE BASICS: GET TO KNOW YOUR PROTECTOR BRAIN AND YOUR WISE MIND

The first thing there is to know about managing intense emotional states has to do with the way the human brain works. A gross oversimplification that can be useful here is to imagine two distinct parts of the brain - not a left side and a right side, but a top and a bottom. The evolutionarily newer, top parts of the brain we'll call the Wise Mind, and the older, bottom parts we'll call the Protector Brain. They function in distinctly different ways, which are discussed more thoroughly in the paragraphs that follow.

The most important part of the Wise Mind is called the Pre-Frontal Cortex (PFC for short). This part of the brain develops through the mid-twenties. It manages the human emotional experience; which means children, teens, and anyone without a fully functional PFC often cannot effectively execute emotion-management strategies. Parents and caregivers can direct the attention of the child in the desired pathways of emotion-regulation, with repetition, until the PFC is fully developed. When activated, the Wise Mind helps people make decisions that are good for us, good for those around us, and good for the planet. The Wise Mind is a creative and flexible problem-solver; therefore learning to activate it before approaching challenges is an important first step in the process.

The Protector Brain, as its name implies, has survival in mind. When it perceives threat - whether physical, emotional, or social - it restricts blood flow from the Wise Mind to keep you safe. It shuts down your digestion, and sends you into fight or flight mode. In some situations too big to fight or flee from, the Protector Brain shuts you down, causing you to "play dead." The Protector Brain plays a very important role. When it works appropriately, it is a literal life-saver.

However, the Protector Brain can create some challenges. One challenge is that it sometimes detects and reacts to situations and cues which are not truly threats. While it happens to everyone, people who have experienced some form of trauma often have more frequent and intense "false" alarms. The Protector Brain also cannot shut itself off, but does respond to cues from the body that the environment is safe and free from danger.

The Protector Brain can be over-reactive in people who:
• experience emotions more intensely than others;
• are shy or more inhibited in social situations;
• react quickly with fear or anxiety when others are calm.
The good news is we can learn coping strategies which help them manage the false alarms and function well.

Questions

1) Recall a time recently when you experienced a takeover by the Protector Brain. What thoughts were you having during that time? Was the threat real or perceived?
2) Recall a time your Protector Brain took over and you were able to soothe it and bring the Wise Mind back online. What strategies did you use?

Experiment

Notice when your Protector Brain gets activated. Draw or write about what happens in your body. Ask people you trust to tell you what they notice, too.

It's actually really interesting. I didn't know we had two different parts of the brain. I mean, I know our brains have different parts, but I didn't know we had a 'smart part' and a 'protector part.' The "Wise Mind" or the smart part does the thinking and your Protector Brain... well, protects you.

It makes sense when you think about it. Like, it was obviously my Protector Brain taking over, forcing me to shut down and retreat into my turtle shell a minute ago. It noticed an emotional threat (my mom was asking me questions, which made my feelings intensify) and I started getting agitated, so it shut me down so I would feel safer. The problem is, it didn't really make me feel better. It just made me feel angrier and more alone, which is why I'm in my room right now, alone, instead of eating at the table.

My mom couldn't get to me in my turtle shell, but I couldn't get to myself either.

But if my Protector Brain was wrong, and shutting down isn't the answer, what is? And why do we have a Protector Brain if it doesn't actually make us feel better? I guess in a life-or-death situation, I would be glad I have a Protector Brain, but in everyday life it's not very useful. The Wise Mind, though - that's definitely useful. I think maybe the trick is to keep the Wise Mind turned on, even when the Protector Brain wants to take over, because the Wise Mind can help you think and work through the problem. It's kind of ironic because all the Protector Brain wants is to help, but by shutting down the Wise Mind it just makes it harder to solve the problem.

CHAPTER 2
i get overwhelmed at an assembly

At the beginning of school, there's an intercom announcement. "Attention," our principal says. "An all-school assembly will be taking place at 12:30 today!"

Great. I hate all-school assemblies. Well, actually I hate all assemblies, but when the whole school is there, it's the worst. It's so loud and boring most of the time. Also, sometimes the 8th graders have to get onstage and give a 30-second speech about their opinion on a topic that the principal gives them, like global warming or something. On the spot! It's supposed to be to "improve our public speaking" and "boost our self-esteem," but it doesn't really work like that. I know 30 seconds doesn't seem long, but when 250-ish kids are staring up at you, most people kind of freeze up.

Anyway, so I spent the morning kind of half listening to the teachers and half trying not to think about the assembly. At lunch, the first free time I get, I pull out The Manual and start reading it, trying to find something to help. I finally just start reading about the Brain-Body Information Highway because it's the second chapter and I've already read the first one, so whatever.

I barely finish the chapter before it's time for the assembly. *Yay.* But I'm armed with Grandpa's words, and it makes me feel more confident.

After suffering through thirty minutes of boredom, the principal points to a random 8th grader (luckily, it's not me) and says, "You, young man, come up here." The kid's name is Derek, and he has to give a speech about "logging." He's one of the "popular" kids, so people will think he's awesome no matter what he says. I'm not like that.

When he's done, the principal chooses another person. And guess what? It's me.

I apparently have to talk about "water conservation." I start to get nervous and shaky before I remember Grandpa's words. At least I remember the general gist of the chapter.

I think about it as I slowly stand up and walk towards the front of the room. What do I remember? The three survival responses are fight, flight and freeze.

What do I feel like doing right now? Freeze - the equivalent of playing dead in front of a predator. I want to freeze up because I'm overwhelmed by everyone watching me give a stupid speech about water conservation. What are the strategies you can use to get over it?

I remember it saying something about repetition. Repetition... repetition... what was that part even referring to? I think it was talking about repeatedly turning on your Wise Mind when you're in a stressful situation, which isn't very helpful right now because I literally have seconds. It also says if you recognize the sensations in your body (which become the messages your body says to your brain), it can calm down your brain. At least I think that's what it says. It's kind of hard to remember quickly while I'm walking to my doom. Well, not literally, but I might as well be. I'm going to make a fool out of myself! I don't have enough time to prepare! My stomach is fluttery and I feel jittery. I'm not ready!

Everyone is looking at me! And talking to each other! It's loud and I start to get overwhelmed. My stomach twists as I remember that everyone will be staring at me even more when I have to talk.

Calm down Jamie. I focus on the feeling of my feet on the floor as I plod up to the stage. I can feel all my weight shift from one foot to the other, inhaling as I lift my foot and exhaling as I set it down. It makes me feel stronger. Calmer. Like I'm a tree that's rooted in the ground. With the part of my brain that's freaking out quieted down, I remember another part of that page in The Manual.

> Once you learn to filter those cues of danger from your body and experiment with the techniques described in this manual, it will take time and repetition to wire up the new pathways in your system. You will no longer immediately believe the thoughts that swirl in your mind; you will learn it is safe to let them settle and begin to make decisions only after the fight, flight, or freeze reaction has passed.

My translation: I need to believe in *myself* instead of the thoughts my Protector Brain makes me think. The Protector Brain wants to scare me enough that I'll give up on the speech and not embarrass myself by messing up in front of the whole school. But - I just realized this - it'll be more embarrassing if I can't do it. There isn't a right or wrong answer, not something I'm supposed to say when I'm up there. It's just my opinion.

Maybe I can make my Protector Brain feel the same way.

It's safe, I think. It doesn't matter what I say.

I just have to do it.

My breathing slows a little and I feel less trembly as I step onto the stage. My nervous feelings haven't totally vanished, but there's a comfort in knowing that I can do it and I don't have much to lose.

"I think that..." My opinion comes easily and I find it's kind of fun to share it. Even if I'm a little quiet and I'm still nervous, I feel good when I'm done. I smile, relieved to be done, but also happy that The Manual's advice worked. I tricked my Protector Brain! I didn't let it take over! I turned on my Wise Mind! I did it!

I remember what it said on the back of The Manual. *Empower your emotions to work for you!* Is this what it meant?

Fight   Flight   Freeze

CHAPTER 3
i lose the manual

Yesterday, my parents decided that after school got out today we were going on a camping trip for the weekend. So now I'm in the car on our way to the campsite.

I like camping. It's so nice and quiet and peaceful, and it feels so good to be in nature. Since I live in the city, it's kind of rare that I get to relax in peace, surrounded by trees. We haven't gone camping very much since my twin sisters were born, but my parents think they're old enough now. I'm not so sure, but I'm going along. They deserve a chance, and I'm not about to turn down a camping trip.

Reading in the car makes me motion-sick, so I stare out the window. We pass a river, which makes me think of water conservation, which makes me think of The Manual.

Wait! The Manual! Did I take it? I know I brought it to school, but did I put it in my backpack as I left? I don't remember! What if I left it at school and it's just sitting in one of the classrooms? The teacher will probably think it's just an old pile of paper and recycle it!

My stomach clenches and curls in on itself. I suddenly feel really hot and sweaty, except my hands, which are cold and sweaty. *Calm down*, I tell myself. *You can find it later. It's okay.* But it doesn't feel okay.

I really, really don't want to lose Grandpa's Manual. I wish he'd managed to get it published before he died. Then maybe this copy wouldn't seem so precious.

I try taking deep breaths but, like before, it doesn't work. Everyone tells you deep breaths are like a cure-all, but that's not true. If I had The Manual right now, I could just read it. I bet it would help me.

But since I don't have The Manual I have to do this on my own.

Okay. I know (kind of) what The Manual would say. First step: turn your Protector Brain OFF and your Wise Mind ON. How do I do that?

Isn't the first part of doing that recognition? Realizing that my Wise Mind is turned off? I did that, but how does it help?

Hang on; I remember part of it! When I read part of this chapter earlier, I remember it said something about moving your eyes around, to reset your brain. Or something along those lines. I think it said the Protector Brain evolved to be aware of what's going on around us so that it can protect us from, for example, a lion attack. So I guess moving your eyes and head around makes the protector brain more at ease.

Where do I look? I move my head in a circle but that just makes me dizzy. Just move my eyes back and forth? That doesn't work either. I start to get annoyed.

Am I over thinking this?

I start moving my eyes and head around. I don't try to distract myself, and I don't think about what I'm doing. I just let my eyes focus on whatever they want to in the car: the steering wheel, the window, my sister's car seat...

In doing so, I feel… calmer. I can feel my shoulders relax and I notice the cool air on my skin. The agitated, stressed part of my brain is turning off, allowing my Wise Mind to take over. Weird to think moving your eyes around can calm you down, but apparently it can.

When the car stops, I jump out and run to the trunk. I pull out my backpack, unzip it… My stomach flutters. What if I did leave it? But I push the thought aside and look into my backpack.

There it is! I'm hit with a wave of relief. So all my stressing was totally useless! Well, not *totally* useless. Some good did come out of it. I mean, I figured out how to stop feeling so stressed! And I did it without The Manual!

I mean, the strategy did come from The Manual, but whatever.

Did it say anything else about the strategy or why it works? I find the page.

SOOTHING THE PROTECTOR BRAIN

The Protector Brain evolved to be aware of our surroundings. This makes sense when you consider our ancestors, who could be eaten if they didn't pay attention to the environment around them. We can use this tool to our advantage today, when we sense that our Protector Brain has been triggered by strong signals in our bodies. Moving the head and eyes from side to side and up and down creates a reward feedback loop which quiets the alerted lower brain systems.

This is not distraction. When you initiate this process, you are not asking the brain to engage in a thought process about anything in the room. You are merely using the turning head and side-to-side eye movements as a mechanism to soothe the lower brain systems.

Since the Protector Brain receives abundant signals from the body, you'll want to become well versed in its language; the language of **sensation**. This is different from the Wise Mind's assignment of labels on the cumulative experience of sensation and thought; what we call **emotion**. There are two types of feelings then; what we actually physically feel with our bodies (which we can call sensation), and what our minds label that experience. To become a master at shifting your emotional experience, you'll need to develop a focused awareness of your internal experience of sensation. Once you become aware of sensations, you can become aware of uncomfortable sensation and shift it into comfortable sensation. Noticing your surroundings is one way to do just that.

Another tool you can use is training yourself to look for and focus on comfortable sensations within your body. Here's how: when you become aware of uncomfortable thoughts or sensations in the body, look for any place on you that feels comfortable and keep your attention there as long as possible. You can also bring to mind a memory of feeling comfortable, keeping your attention on the memory until you feel it in your body and can focus on the sensation.

I was right about the eye-moving. The Protector Brain, in the words of The Manual, "evolved to be aware of our surroundings," so if you move your eyes around, it tells your Protector Brain you're safe because you don't see a threat (even if the threat is internal, like being stressed about, say, LOSING SOMETHING, and you can't actually see it).

It was also interesting to me to read the part about feelings and sensations. Apparently, they're two different things. A sensation is something you physically feel in your body, like when I felt hot, and a feeling is what our brain calls it when we combine sensation and thought. Like when my stomach clenched and my palms got sweaty (sensation) and I started thinking I'd lost The Manual (thought). The sensation and the thought combined to make a feeling - stressed, or worried.

Now that I'm not stressed, I try the experiment.

> Practice noticing what's around you for the first few times when your Protector Brain is not activated. You're establishing a new neural pathway and strengthening it (like a muscle) so it's much easier to do when you start feeling overwhelmed. Start by scanning your body, from your feet up to your head, and notice any sensations that are present. Rate both your level of discomfort and your level of comfort on separate scales of 1-10 (they won't necessarily add up to equal 10). Notice what's around you, making sure to turn your head at a comfortable pace to look in various directions, and do this several times at a comfortable pace. Assess sensation in your body by scanning feet to head again, and rate the levels of discomfort and comfort again. Note any changes.

I lean against a tree. I'm supposed to notice sensations. I'm happy, but is that a sensation? I don't think so. It's a feeling. My arms are kind of tense, but the sun is warming my skin and it feels good. My level of comfort is probably nine. I don't know why it's not 10, but it's not. Nine feels right, and I don't need to justify it because these are my feelings, and this is my journal. So nine it is.

What's around me? I see lots of really tall green trees. Also campsites. Both of the ones next to us are empty, but across from us, there's an older couple setting up a dark red tent. I also see birds flying in a V. It's really pretty and quiet. Even my sisters are being good. They're happy to be out of the car.

Now I'm supposed to assess my sensations again. All of my muscles feel loose and relaxed now. My level of discomfort is still 0, but my level of comfort is 10. I'm peaceful and relaxed from my head to my toes.

CHAPTER 4
my little sisters ruin my drawing

I CANNOT BELIEVE THEM!!! I leave my journal on my desk for FIVE MINUTES and they draw all over my sketch of Grandpa! HOW COULD THEY? I am SO MAD RIGHT NOW and my parents don't even care that my sisters RUINED that picture! They had NO RIGHT to snoop in my notebook. I did NOTHING to them! I'm just glad they didn't find -

Wait. WHAT IF THEY FOUND GRANDPA'S MANUAL? If they did something to it, I will NEVER FORGIVE THEM! I run to my desk and open the third drawer down. It's not here!!! Did I put it in the drawer yesterday? I'm frantic. Where is it???

Hang on; it's right there. Good.

I have a moment of relief before remembering my journal. Then I get angry all over again. My stupid sisters!!! I was going to frame that picture and hang it on the wall! Then I would have something to remember Grandpa by other than his manual -

Wait, his manual! Maybe there's something in there about, I don't know, maybe OVERCOMING YOUR ANGER AT YOUR HORRIBLE, EVIL SIBLINGS WHO MESS UP YOUR DRAWINGS AND DESTROY ALL YOUR STUFF!!! Ugg, I am going to KILL THEM…

Grandpa's Manual probably doesn't say anything about making death threats, though. I almost laugh, but I'm still too angry for anything other than anger to penetrate my brain. All other thoughts and feelings just bounce off the shield my anger set up. Nothing can come in, but nothing (like my anger) can go out either.

I open the manual, trying to collect my thoughts. Table of Contents. Play with Your Intense Emotions? Well, anger is definitely an intense emotion…

There's a questions section, and I skip to it because none of the information is sticking in my brain. Right at the moment I need a solution. I don't need to know why that solution worked. Maybe I'll read the science part later.

> Think about a situation where you felt overwhelmingly frustrated. Where does that frustration live in your body? What does it physically feel like? Use sensory language from the previous chapter to describe it.

Okay. A situation where I felt super frustrated? Easy. That's now. But what's the book talking about? Frustration doesn't LIVE somewhere. It's a feeling. It's in your whole body. Right?

I guess I never really thought about this. Do feelings have certain homes, places in your body? If the Manual says they do, maybe it's true. I mean, it's been right so far.

I close my eyes. I always think best when I close my eyes. Closing my eyes kind of shuts off my useless thoughts, so I can focus on the important ones.

Okay. I'm pretty much totally sure that my anger lives in my hands and arms. When I imagine being angry, my hands and arms clench up, all the way up to my shoulders.

They get all tight and full of energy, like a spring that's ready to release. I guess it makes sense for my energy to be in my hands, because that's what I draw with. But I've never tried drawing while I'm angry. It never even occurred to me that drawing might be a better outlet than yelling or shutting myself in my room.

Would it be? I'm trying it. I'm curious now.

I cross the room and pick up my sketchbook. Then I hear the door open behind me. My mom must be coming in to talk to me now that I've "cooled down." She knows it won't be productive if I'm still angry. You know, a heart-to-heart conversation where I tell her what's wrong, she fixes it, we hug, and we're done. That kind of talk.

Except I'm sort of fixing the issue already, with Grandpa's help.

"Hey, Peanut," she says.

"Mom!" I say. "Don't call me Peanut. That was my baby nickname. I'm a teen now."

She laughs, and her eyes land on the Manual, now spread all over the floor. I really need to staple the pages together or something. I'm getting tired of picking them up.

"What's this?" she says as she bends down to pick it up.

I don't know why, but I got really panicked when I saw her reaching for it. "Mom!"

"What?"

"That's Grandpa's Manual. You know, the one he wrote that never got published? The one he left for me before he-" I can't say it. It's been five years and I still can't say it. But she understands.

I don't know how to say it, so I just say it. "Mom, can you, uh, leave? I was kind of about to start drawing."

"Oh," she says. "Okay." And she turns around and leaves.

I love my mom. So much. But she's not like me. She loves small talk and conversation. She thrives in crowds and groups. She's an extrovert through and through. I work better on my own. I get overwhelmed easily by large groups and lots of noise.

Moving on. I pick up the page of The Manual I was reading and set it on my desk with the sketchpad. My fingers hover over the blank page for a minute, but my mind is empty. I can't think of anything I want to draw.

I resort to looking at the next question in The Manual.

2. What color is associated with that frustration? Don't come up with an answer, simply ask yourself the question and accept the first color that comes to mind. You may actually see the color in your imagination, or the answer might come to you another way. Be open.

Duh, I think. Anger. I'm going to think of the color red. But I close my eyes again and ask myself the question.

What color is associated with that frustration?

And I get - nothing. Nothing. My brain is still empty of anything. I try to force a color into my mind but it doesn't feel right. I'm an artist. A color should come to me. Maybe if I open my eyes?

The first thing I see is my green bedspread. But green stays in my mind. I know that's not the right color, though, because green makes me feel calm, not angry. I'm restless. It's not working! The Manual doesn't lie. Why can't I just think of a simple color?

I move from a sitting position to a standing one and close my eyes again. Instead of thinking of red, or green, or any color, I think of frustration. *Anger.* I remember what it's like to be angry. And I feel - don't see, but feel - a deep eggplant purple-y color. I didn't know it was possible to imagine a color without seeing it. I didn't know you could feel colors.

> 3. Now, imagine taking that frustration out of your body and putting it on the chair next to you. What shape is the frustration? Does it have smooth or rough edges; solid lines or fuzzy; and is it moving or does it stay still? How big is it? Describe it in as much detail as possible. Write it down or draw it, using the color you found in the previous section. You may discover new colors as you elaborate on the details.

I feel sort of weird, but no one's watching, so why not? I actually, physically, pretend to suck the anger out of my arms and drop it on the chair next to me. It's weird. I could almost feel it.

Now I know what to draw. My anger. It flows out of my pencil like it was trapped inside, waiting to get out. It doesn't look at all like I was expecting. I guess I thought it would be a red, pointy thing. But it's really more of an eggplant-colored ball covered in really short pieces of string that look like nubs. It's sort of fuzzy looking. Not fuzzy really, but soft. Like a pom pom. Like something a cat would play with.

Like something that might WANT to be noticed and played with. Which I guess is what I'm doing right now. I'm the cat.

> 4. Make that frustration into a character. Is it masculine, or feminine? Does it have facial features? What might its name be? Perhaps the most important question is: What does it want, and why?

Wait, so now my anger is a PERSON? This is getting weird. How am I supposed to know its name, much less what it wants?

Hold on. I already know what it wants. I seriously wrote it just a minute ago. It wants to be noticed. If you think about it, anger isn't really noticed. We either push it down or try to shove it out (by yelling, punching, slamming doors, you know - venting). And since now I know what it wants, I should be able to figure out a name. Oh, whatever. I'm not good at naming things and I can't think of any names that fit. I'm moving on to the next question.

> 5. What other feelings and thoughts might you like to create characters out of? Worries, fears, anger, rage, sadness, bitterness, even happiness?

It would be weird to make characters out of a happy feeling, wouldn't it? I mean, why would you? Happy feelings don't need processing, do they? Not like anger does.

It's funny, I had kind of forgotten I was even angry. I'm calm now. Being aware of my anger and noticing it made me calm down and let my Wise Mind take over to solve the problem in a better way. I mean, I totally could have done what I normally do (yelling at someone, then slamming my door and sulking) but instead, I worked through the problem with my Wise Mind.

CHAPTER 5
i get worried about art club

"Hey, Jamie," my mom says when she picks me up from school. Am I being paranoid, or is she being fake casual? You know, how parents sometimes have this weird tone in their voice, and don't look exactly at you, like they're worried you're going to freak out or something? Is my mom the only parent who does this?

Maybe I should start over.

"Hey, Jamie," my mom says super-casually when she picks me up from school. "I got an email today from your principal -"

The principal? Why would she be emailing my mom? Unless - wait, what if someone reported me for reading The Manual during class? It was only once, in math, when I was waiting for help, but still. I don't want to get in trouble!

My mom must see me panicking because she says, "Jamie. Calm down. It was sent to all the parents, you know, the whole 8th-grade class. There's an art club starting after school! Isn't that great?"

I hesitate. I do love art, but I do not love people. I mean, I'm not super antisocial or anything, but I definitely prefer being alone to being in a big group of annoying eighth-grade kids. "I guess," I finally say unenthusiastically, mostly because I don't want to say no. And who knows? Maybe it'll be fun.

"Great!" Mom says. "It's on Tuesdays. It says in the email to bring your best piece of work to the first meeting. There's a contest! The best piece of art gets to be in the yearbook! Isn't that exciting, honey?"

Tuesday? That's tomorrow! Wait. A contest? My stomach twists. I do NOT like competing. Not if I'm not sure I'll win.

I mostly forget about it all until nighttime, when I'm lying in bed. I don't know about you, but that's when my worries all worm their way sneakily into my brain. A picture comes into my head - me, drawing at my desk. It makes me feel happy until I remember art club is tomorrow! I don't have a "best work" chosen yet? Will I have time tomorrow before school? Will the teacher get mad at me if I don't bring art?

What if we have to introduce ourselves and I freeze up in front of the whole club? Or start mumbling so no one can hear me? Everyone will stare at me! My stomach clenches up at the thought.

I don't usually have much trouble sleeping, but I have bags under my eyes the next day. I sleep through my alarm and have to get ready super fast. At the last second, I remember the art club, so I grab the first sketchpad I see and hope it has something good enough to show people.

I spend first period (algebra) obsessing over that stupid sketchpad burning a hole in my bag, and I can't concentrate in second or third periods either. The second the bell announces the start of lunch break, I pull the sketchpad out of my bag and critically examine each drawing. Colors that seemed right now seem too bright or too pale and all my drawings look bad.

I can't choose. I hate all my drawings now that I have to show them to someone. Why did I agree to this art club?

I won't go. I'll call my mom and tell her I don't want to. That unties the knot in my stomach a little bit, but it makes me feel like a chicken. Honestly, I'm kind of disappointed in myself.

Right after school ends, I step into a hallway to call my mom. My fingers are sweaty as I dial her number and push Talk. What is she going to think of me?

I try to sound relaxed and normal, not on the edge of a breakdown, when she answers.

"Hello?"

"Hi, Mom. It's, um, me. Jamie." (Did I mention I'm not good at talking on phones? I either get tongue-tied and trip over my words, or I talk too fast.)

"Jamie! Is something wrong?"

"Not really. I just, um, decided that... Idon'twanttogotoartclub. So can you come pick me up?"

"Honey? Why?" My mom sounds disappointed. Shouldn't it be ME that's disappointed, not her? It's ME that's missing out on something, not her.

"I don't know, I just don't. Is that okay? Can you please just pick me up?" I feel like a baby, like I'm going to start crying.

"Of course I can. Can you wait outside for a minute?"

"Okay, Mom. Love you. Bye."

I hang up feeling worse than I had before. Why can't I do anything right?

When I get home, I go to my room to sulk. I don't know what I'm sulking about, but I do know that I'm in one of those moods where nothing sounds fun. I try to imagine what I would be doing right now if I had gone to art club. Whatever that Jamie is doing probably beats moping around, yet that's all I feel like doing. It's weird how being grumpy is satisfying, in a way.

But after about five minutes I get bored of being grumpy, and too bored to be stubborn. (Sometimes I get in a mood where I feel like I should be grumpy even when I don't actually want to, and I'm too stubborn to give up and be un-grumpy.) Since I'm super bored, I open my bottom desk drawer (this drawer is getting a lot of use since I found The Manual) and pull out Grandpa's dusty pile of pages.

I saw a chapter earlier that I think might work. Something about fears? Oh, there it is! *Make Friends with your Fears!*

MAKE FRIENDS WITH YOUR FEARS

Worries and fears share one thing in common: activation of the Protector Brain. They often represent a belief about physical, emotional, or social safety in our world. The Protector Brain can't distinguish between a perceived threat ("maybe I will feel embarrassed") or a real one (being chased by a tiger), so any threat cues detected by the brain can trip the alarm. As we've previously established, once this occurs, blood flow from the wiser parts of the brain becomes restricted to the survival mechanism. Then we can feel worry, which has physiological components similar to the fight/flight energetic survival strategy, or fear, often associated with the freeze strategy. To create a different neural network for perceived threats, it is important to work with them when you are in a safe, protected space; physically, emotionally, and socially.

Often, our initial response to worry/fear is to push it down, look away, and avoid it as much as possible. This may work temporarily as we become distracted, but without resolution the worry/fear continues to wield power over our mental worlds. When we truly understand this, we can find inspiration to find a safe venue to meet this fear and discover what it's so afraid of. Once we do this, we can use our Wise Minds to think of creative solutions which address the fear and allow us to be in choice about how to move forward.

Questions

1) What are some situations that are real, actual threats? What situations are better classified as perceived (ie, no physical threat to life)?
2) What behaviors, thoughts, and/or sensations clue you in that you are experiencing worry? Does that align with a high-energy state of repetitive thinking, a need to move, or easily-irritated by others?

3) What behaviors, thoughts, and/or sensations clue you in that you are experiencing fear? Do you experience a low-energy state of absent or stuck thinking, a physical inability to move, and desire to either isolate or cling to someone?
4) What people, places, and/or strategies help you feel safe? (Refer back to Soothing the Protector Brain if you get stuck!)

Experiment

The first step is to create safety for yourself. Choose a place that is very comfortable for you. You might like to collect some of your favorite things to look at or touch. Take a few moments to look around, noticing the environment around you. You may ask someone you trust to help you with this, or complete it on your own.

Next, choose the worry or fear you'd like to work with. Imagine it as a character, separate from you. What does it look like? How does it move (or not)? Where is it in relationship to you? What would you name it? Draw or write about it to really help it separate from you. If you become overwhelmed at any point in this experiment, shift your attention back to the place and things that are comfortable to you, and stay there as long as you'd like. When you feel ready, come back to the experiment. You might find that you would like to have someone comforting present with you, and you can ask them to simply be in the room with you or be close to you without asking questions about your experiment yet.

Now, ask the worry or fear what it wants. The first answer you get may not be the best fit - question the worry/fear until you discover what it's trying to protect you from. All worries and fears activate our Protector Brains to protect us from something. What is this worry or fear you've chosen trying to protect you from?

Can you accept the genuine desire of this worry/fear to protect you? Can you see the good place of intention it comes from? Let the worry/fear character know you understand where it's coming from. You can draw this on your paper, write about it, or imagine it in your mind. Tell the worry/fear that your wise self has got this concern under control, so the worry/fear can rest now.

The last step is deciding how to move forward where the worry/fear has ruled your behavior and thoughts. How would you like to handle this situation?

I don't know why I didn't read this earlier. It makes so much sense to learn about the science behind feelings to help understand (and overcome) them. I really like this chapter because it's sort of like an extension of the last one. I mean, in the last chapter I made a character out of my anger (which I know isn't the same as fear, but it's an emotion), and in this chapter I'm supposed to get to know it. I never really thought fears had a purpose until I read Chapter 1 of The Manual, which explains about how the Protector Brain tries to keep you alive and safe. The annoying thing about it is the Protector Brain sometimes thinks something is threatening (like art club) when really it probably would have been fine. I mean, I wouldn't have died or anything. So why did my Protector Brain prevent me from going to art club, where I could have met people and had fun? I keep reading.

It says here that if you can find out what your fear is so afraid of, it allows your Wise Mind to work on a solution and find ways to move past the fear. That would be helpful if I knew how to talk to my own emotions. Although isn't that what I did with the last chapter of the book?

I guess our fears want to keep us safe, but from what? There was no physical threat from going to art club. Safe from feeling embarrassed?

From failing in some way?

I think that's more accurate than anything else. I didn't want to fail. Or more accurately, I didn't want other people to think I failed. That I was a bad artist. I wanted them to accept me.

So my fear was trying to protect me from the disappointment I would have felt if the other people in the club didn't like my drawings, or if the club didn't live up to my expectations. That makes sense, but it also makes me feel sad. I could have gone anyway if I'd known this before. I would have been fine if I had just tried to process my fear, instead of shoving it away.

Fears try to keep you safe, at the cost of having fun.

CHAPTER 6
i can't decide what to buy

My birthday was yesterday! Happy birthday to me! I'm 14 now. I don't feel any different, though. I don't look different either, which isn't surprising. I mean, it's not like you age extra on your birthday or something. And 14 isn't exactly a milestone birthday. But it's still exciting, even though I didn't have a party or anything like that. It's not that I'm too old. Actually, I think a party would be fun. But my friends don't agree (they think birthday parties are too immature for teenagers) and what fun is a party if no one comes? That's kind of the point.

Anyway, my parents gave me money so I could buy whatever I wanted. I'm at a clothes store right now and I CANNOT DECIDE what to get.

I'm a pretty good decision maker. At least, I think I am. I don't normally regret my decisions, but it takes me a LONG time to decide on things. I'm one of those people who has to look through the whole store a few times before narrowing down their options, then deliberates intensely on what to get. It takes forever, but at least I'm usually happy with what I end up choosing.

Sadly, that isn't the case this time. I've narrowed it down to a green beanie, rainbow striped socks, a dark blue polo shirt, or a new pair of jeans. I could get both the beanie and the socks, or the polo shirt, or the jeans. But I cannot for the life of me choose.

I only have about 10 minutes before my mom comes to pick me up. And I don't know what to choose. They're all good choices, and I would probably be happy with any of them. Do I need new jeans? Not really, but they're comfortable. I almost always wear polo shirts, though, so that would be a safe bet. My grandpa used to wear polos, so it would also remind me of him. But I don't really need another polo shirt either. Come to think of it, I also don't need a beanie or socks. So I'm back at square one.

Great.

I'm not panicking, but I'm getting seriously annoyed at myself. Apparently, I'm incapable of making a simple decision. If my mom comes back and I still haven't chosen anything she'll probably get annoyed too.

I look at the clock. 5 minutes left. I just need to choose something.

The socks and beanie are more... I don't know, bold than what I usually wear. And I have lots of jeans. So I'll just go with the polo shirt - boring, but safe. It's a good choice. Right?

Mom comes in as I'm standing in line. "Jamie!" She joins me in line. "What did you decide on?"

I show her the shirt. "This shirt," I say, kind of defensively. My mom looks like she's about to respond, but she doesn't. Instead of giving her opinion, she obviously thinks that I'm old enough to make my own choices.

Which is a good thing. I'm glad she trusts my judgment. Because I also trust my judgment. Especially when it comes to making spur-of-the-moment choices.

We're second from the front of the line. I'm nervous for some reason. I force myself to rethink my choice. Am I happy with my choice? *Yes*, my thinking brain says. But the rest of my brain is silent. It's quiet because it's afraid to voice its opinion.

You can talk now, I say to my instinct brain. *You have permission. Tell me what you think.*

It's kind of weird to talk to your own brain, but it works. The thoughts of my brain come out of hiding. No, not the thoughts. The feelings.

And the rest of my brain isn't sure about the shirt. It's just like every shirt I own. Is that a good thing? I can't decide.

I step out of line, ducking under the rope barrier things. What are those even called? Oh, whatever. It doesn't matter.

I feel like The Manual would help me now. I really should start carrying it around. Or maybe I should type up another copy or something, a smaller one that I actually could carry around. That would be helpful.

Then I remember - I was reading The Manual in the car! I walk over to my mom and ask her for the car keys. "I need to get The Manual."

She laughs and pulls it out of the bag she's carrying. "I had a feeling you would need it." She smiles. So do I. My mom knows me well.

I retreat to a (relatively) quiet corner and open to where I left off. I scan the page, and when I see the word 'decision-making' I know this is the right page for the situation.

ACCESSING THE WISDOM WITHIN

Built within our nervous/sensory systems exists an internal tuning fork; a directional nudge towards that which is most life-affirming for us. We can learn to tap into this inner resource as an additional authority in our decision-making processes.

Using sensory cues and mental images, you can develop this muscle of inner wisdom. It requires a moment of balance and void of perceived threats which would activate the Protector Brain. The Wise Mind has connections to the nervous system which allow us to have an awareness of what's arising in our internal landscape, versus the connections of the Protector Brain which merely subject us to it's variety of survival reactions.

Sensory cues may come in the form of movement, temperature, sound, texture, and pressure. Some people get sensory information in the form of an image or perception of sound.

Questions

1) Think of situations where you have felt unclear about the best choice to make. What strategies did you employ to look for answers?
2) Have you ever "just known" the right answer or choice for you? How?
3) Read the following words aloud and note the reaction in your body:

NO   NO   NO   NO

NO   NO   NO

4) Now read this set of words aloud and note your internal reaction:

Yes   Yes   Yes   Yes

Yes   Yes!   Yes!

Experiment

Get comfortable in a quiet, emotionally/socially/physically safe place. Quiet your thinking brain (try closing your eyes) and go inside of yourself. Attune to your physical experience as you sit or lie on the floor, chair, or your bed.

Say NO to yourself firmly ten times, as in question 3 above. Identify the sensations, colors, images, shape, and movement your internal experience reacts with. Repeat this process saying YES, noting the sensory reaction you have. You can write or draw these reactions in a journal to help you remember.

Now that you have identified two ends of your tuning fork, test it out. State a very basic, simple truth that is an absolute yes (you can try "my name is _____"). Notice the sensory reaction. Is it a match to the reaction you had for question 4? Now play with something which you feel strongly to be untrue. Note your sensory reaction.

Once you are getting consistent sensory reactions to questions you feel confident are either true or untrue, you can being testing this internal tuning fork in more challenging situations. Remember to always ground yourself in a safe space before attempting to navigate this experiment.

Let's see. I think I'll try the questions and then the experiment. That will probably help me.

Think of situations where you have felt unclear about the best choice to make. What strategies did you employ to look for answers?

When I was trying to decide on the clothes, I thought about what I would use most and what I already had. It didn't really work, though. Normally I do the same thing, and it works fine. Like, I don't need to buy something I already have or something I think I'll never, ever use. That's just common sense.

Have you ever "just known" the right answer or choice for you? How?

Not really. I mean, I've always thought through things instead of just going with whatever my original opinion was.

But haven't I known some things for sure? Like what to draw? I never need help deciding that. I draw whatever feels right.

How do I define the "right" choice? That's what the question is really saying. I guess I think of the right choice as something that makes me happy.

This is a hard question. Moving on.

Read the following words aloud and note the reaction in your body:

NO   NO   NO   NO

NO   NO   NO

So I'm supposed to read things aloud? In a store crowded with teens? Whatever. It's not like someone I know will be here. Probably. Actually, the chance of me seeing someone from school at this store is really high. So I decide to just read it in my head.

NO! I silently yell in a mean voice. That's what the word sounds like in my head. *NO! NO! NO! NO!*

I'm too self-conscious to close my eyes (that would look really weird) but I try only to focus on how I feel. Just thinking the word NO makes me tense up and my breathing gets faster. My teeth clench and I breathe in sharp puffs out my nose. I feel like an angry bull that's about to charge someone. Also, I see flashes of orange in my mind's eye. Weird.

> Now read this set of words aloud and note your internal reaction:
>
> Yes   Yes   Yes   Yes
>
> Yes   Yes!   Yes!

I use the same strategy. When my head fills with yes's, I relax a little, and soft yellow pulses in my mind's eye. It reminds me of a hybrid sun/heart. It's moving like a heart, pulsing with the rhythm of my breaths, but it looks and feels like a sun. Calm, comfortable… I think of warm sand on the beach and laying in the grass on a hot summer day.

It's funny that thinking words can make your body react so strongly.

I don't think I need to try the experiment. I have the tools I need. No is orange flashes and anger; Yes is yellow light and contentment. Got it.

I go back to my purchases. One by one, I hold them in my hands and imagine myself leaving with them.

The jeans are automatically out. I feel a strong NO and I don't bother to justify it, just set them back on the shelf. The shirt is a little more ambiguous because I almost bought it before. I have a harder time relaxing and feeling what I really feel, but I tense up and feel grumpy when I think about taking them up to the stand again. So those are a no.

Which leaves the beanie and socks, but I might not want them both. I'm not sure about either of them. They caught my eye, but I don't really know why. They're brighter than what I normally wear.

I go to a dressing room - even though I already tried on the hat I couldn't see myself. I smile when I see it on my head. It makes me feel cozy and energetic at the same time (I didn't know that was even possible!) so I say YES.

The socks are trickier. I hold them in my hands and they don't scream yes or no. So I imagine myself buying the hat and leaving the socks on the shelf, which makes me feel sad and droopy. I picture myself wearing them and close my eyes, and see yellow light. Yes.

This time, I don't duck out of line. At the last second, I see a cool black bracelet and grab it. I have just enough to buy it, the beanie, and the socks. I don't need to deliberate for an hour on it this time. I just picture myself wearing it, close my eyes and feel yellow light. Happiness. That's all the validation I need.

We walk out of the store. I feel lighter than a balloon and happy with my purchases. "What are those rope barrier things called?" I ask my mom. I'm in a chatty mood.

"What rope barrier things?"

"The ones that... oh, never mind." I laugh, and pretty soon we're both laughing, and I feel happier than I've been in a while.

"You know what, Mom?" I say. "I've decided I want a birthday party this year. Just with a few friends. Is that okay?"

She's surprised. "Sure, Peanut. But didn't you say just last week that parties are for little kids?"

I let her use of my nickname slip. "Yeah, but I realized that's what my friends think. Not me. I've learned to trust my judgment."

CHAPTER 7
my friend makes me feel bad about my test score

"Hey Jamie," my friend says to me as my teacher passes our math tests back. "What score did you get?"

"Score?" I say, confused. A second later I feel really embarrassed, and my face turns red. "Oh. Duh. *That* score."

"I got an 82!"

"Oh. Good for you." I personally got an 89, but I'm not about to say that.

"Mia probably got a better score than you, though," he says matter-of-factly. "She got a 97! How can you beat that?"

I don't really care about what score Mia got, but it would probably be rude to walk away so I just pretend to listen. When I don't respond, my friend grabs my arm. "Aren't you jealous?"

"No, not really."

"You should be! How is she the best at everything? It's so unfair!"

I'm still not really jealous, but I guess he has a point. Even though my Wise Mind knows she probably just studies more, the rest of my brain, which is starting to get annoyed at Mia, overrides it. My mood switches at light speed. Why is she always the best? Am I just dumber than her? I don't know. A B+ is pretty good, but I'm jealous anyway. Why didn't I try harder? Why did Mia have to do so well?

I'm grumpy for the rest of the day. I don't know if it's because Mia got a 97 or if it's because my friend pointed it out to me, but I feel like I failed, even though I got a B+. Still, I can't change my feelings. It's too late now.

When I get home, my mom asks me what's wrong.

"I got an 89 on my test," I say grumpily.

"Why is that a bad thing?" my mom asks. I don't have an answer that I want to give her. Saying "I'm grumpy because someone got a better score than me" sounds really petty. I'm not the best student in my class anyway. There's always someone who gets a better grade than me. Why am I upset now?

You know why, a little annoying voice says in my head. *Because your friend pointed it out. He was jealous of Mia. He told you that you didn't do as well as she did. His jealousy rubbed off on you or something.* But I'm too embarrassed to admit that to my mom. I'm too embarrassed to admit it to myself.

Since I still haven't answered my mom, she says sort of snippily,

"Well, if you're not going to talk about it, you should go to your room and read that manual that Grandpa left you."

Actually, that's a good idea. I go up to my room and start looking at the table of contents. The Impact of the Intense Emotional States of Others sounds like it might fit this situation…

THE IMPACT OF THE INTENSE
EMOTIONAL STATES OF OTHERS

Neuroception is a term coined by Dr. Stephen Porges. It describes a subconscious system for detecting threats and safety. As we have seen, the Protector Brain does not distinguish between an actual life-threatening situation vs. a perceived emotional threat. Our systems have subconscious means of detecting these perceived types of social/emotional threats as a way of keeping us safe from embarrassment, emotional vulnerability, and other emotional deaths.

One example of how it does this is via electromagnetic signal detection. The Institute of HeartMath found that the electromagnetic signal emitted from the heart is detectable up to three feet around it. Heart signals tell us when a person is feeling a negative, threatened state (emotional correlates include frustration or anger), and also when they're feeling a positive, safe, balanced state (emotionally translated as appreciation or gratitude).

Knowing this, we become aware of the impact of others on our own internal state. For example, if you're feeling okay and a person with an agitated state enters your radius of detection, your survival mechanisms react and become activated, creating a type of alarm within you. It makes sense if you think of humans as a herd of sorts. The herd's survival depends on detecting outside threat, and the individual's survival depends on attunement to the herd. It's important to remember that survival activation does not differentiate between physical, emotional, social, nor real vs. perceived threats. A perceived embarrassment in front of peers activates a survival reaction similarly to a lion on the savannah. It's a life-changing realization.

Another empowering piece of information is that our signals impact others, too. When we notice someone in a threatened state, we can intentionally tune into ourselves, create a sense of ease, balance, and gratitude within us, and impact the physiology of the other person. It's a powerful tool when you want to help someone but aren't sure what to say, and for those times you are in disagreement with another and it's going downhill. Often, words alone aren't enough.

Questions

1) Can you recall a time where someone else seemed to impact you on this subconscious level? Maybe they were frustrated or irritated about something else, and you could feel it inside of yourself? Or perhaps you've had the opposite experience, where someone's calm and gentle presence helped you release frustration.
2) How do you experience frustration in your physical body? Remember to use sensory language like color, shape, movement, and texture.
3) How do you experience gratitude in your body?
4) What tools help you get into a state of gratitude, thereby helping you emit positive electromagnetic signals into the space around you?

Experiment

Work through the questions above. Draw or write your answers down and compare. What are the differences? Play with initiating the state of gratitude by bringing to mind a time you felt loved or loving. Imagine the scene as fully as you can, bringing to mind any sounds, sights, scents, and sensations you experienced. Stay there for as long as is comfortable, for at least several minutes. Pay special attention to any sensations you experience around your heart area; perhaps a lightness or warmth that radiates out.

Next, think of a situation you've had feelings of frustration or irritation about. Think about this for a few moments and notice how your body sensations shift. Now let go of that situation and those feelings and turn your attention back to the state of gratitude. See if you can make it as big as it was before. Congratulations - you have demonstrated being able to change your emotional state without anything in your environment shifting!

Now pay attention to your state when you are in close proximity to others. Try to generate a state of gratitude anytime you think of it - for your benefit, and for those around you!

Here's what I learned from the chapter: apparently you *can* change your emotions, and use them as a tool to soothe people if their feelings are negative. Also, we pick up on other people's emotions, like how when my friend was jealous of Mia's score and it made me jealous too, which made me grumpy. I guess it would be helpful for wild animals if they were in a herd and one was scared because it sensed an attack or something. It would be a warning. But people can talk. And feelings can lie.

That's one thing The Manual has taught me - sometimes your brain makes up feelings when it thinks you're in danger, which can make you feel bad. And most of the time you're not really in danger. You have to get past them.

But feelings can be important too, and helpful. If you don't pay attention to your feelings and sensations, you lose information about yourself, and you lose the chance to grow. But if you pay too much attention to your feelings you can hurt other people, and yourself, and it makes you more unhappy.

I understand now that I let myself get jealous. I should have just ended the conversation and walked away before my friend made me pick up on his emotions. But I also should have checked The Manual before and followed the advice I'd already read. I could have changed my mood if I'd tried. I could have opened myself up and let my mom's or my friend's good mood rub off on me. But I didn't.

I've learned something interesting: Feelings can be transmitted, so if you're in a bad mood it can rub off on other people. That's one of the reasons why it's important to be open and to change your mood.

CHAPTER 8
my sister interrupts me while i'm drawing

I'm sitting at my desk, sketching a new picture of Grandpa, when my little sister comes into my room. She doesn't knock. I don't like it when people don't knock.

"Jamie, come down for dinner!" she sings.

"Okay, Kylie. Be down in a minute." I really want to finish my drawing, but I can't keep working with her in the room.

She doesn't leave. "Dad says not to come down unless I bring you with me."

Ugggg, I think, but out loud I say, "One MINUTE! I'm trying to FINISH this!!!" Which sounds ruder than I meant it to, and she looks hurt. But I really want to keep going before dinner. I'm in a drawing zone, and after dinner, I might not be.

"That was mean," my sister says sadly, looking down at the floor, her pigtails drooping. I feel ashamed, but also defiant and angry. It's not a good mix, because I feel angry about my sister making me feel ashamed, which makes me feel even more ashamed because she doesn't deserve my anger. It's a vicious cycle.

She's right, that little truthful voice whispers in my ear. *That was mean. Say sorry.*

But I don't want to say sorry. I'm too stubborn for that, and besides, I wasn't in a bad mood until she interrupted me. Now I'm mad, and it's all her fault.

You can change your mood, the voice nags. *The Manual taught you how.* But I don't want to change my mood. I'm allowed to be mad sometimes. And SHE shouldn't be allowed to barge in and interrupt me. Why didn't Dad just come in and get me himself? Why can't I just draw in peace for ONE MORE MINUTE?

"GET OUT!" I yell. "Leave me alone!" My fists clench and unclench. It crosses my mind to try drawing (it worked last time I was angry) but the angry part of my brain just wants to stay angry. It's stubborn, and even though being angry isn't rewarding, it's kind of satisfying in a twisted way.

She starts crying, but she leaves. Now that she's gone, I feel really bad. The anger's passed and I fight back tears. I should have followed The Manual's advice. If I had, my sister wouldn't have left my room crying and I would be downstairs, much happier than I am now.

I'm too much of a coward to go down now that I made my sister so sad, but I feel like a horrible person. Why did I get angry? For me, anger leads to sadness a lot, because I almost always regret what I did when I was angry. So if being angry makes me feel bad, why did I let myself get angry? And stay angry? I have the tools now to get over my anger. Why didn't I?

I already wrote the answer. Because it's satisfying to get angry once in a while. Because it's hard to always keep your emotions bottled up. But there are other ways to release your anger, ways that don't hurt other people. Physically or emotionally.

I'm not mad anymore, but I am sad. Didn't I see a page in The Manual about family relationships or something? It might help me.

HOW AND WHY IT'S IMPORTANT TO HAVE HEALTHY AND HELPFUL RELATIONSHIPS

The short, simple answer to why it's important to have relationships (whether healthy or not, turns out) is that they help us learn and grow into the best versions of ourselves that can be. If one lives in isolation, they limit the number of ways their brain can expand and take in new possibilities. This expansion of thought and awareness of multiple solutions to problems leads to increased happiness in life. These experiences also widen our window of tolerance, meaning we learn new skills which help us overcome new and varying obstacles.

It's important to have healthy relationships because we learn by experience. If we do not get the parenting that we need to be happy and resilient when we are children, we truly must experience love and support from another person before we can fully know it ourselves and pass it on to others around us. We also develop inner language based on what we hear around us. If we hear "don't be sad, smile" our whole childhood, and never experience another person being okay with our sadness, then we can develop that inner dismissive language ourselves into adulthood. Many parents mean well and simply have never been shown the way to be the parents they truly want to be.

Some of us are born impacted by those around us in more overwhelming ways than most others. It becomes too risky to reach out for support, because the other person can easily add to our internal chaos without meaning to. Those of us who feel this way have two options; shrink away and shut ourselves off from others, or learn how to ask for the specific support we are needing to regain balance. It's of neurological benefit for us to do this; our nervous system is wired to soothe when engaged with non-threatening-feeling others (see the work of Stephen Porges for more detailed information). In other words, we can activate our Wise Minds, think more clearly, and better problem solve our challenges when we activate the relational dynamic in the midst of our internal chaos. It's not about the other person's words or wisdom at all - it's merely the effects of having a calm, grounded person in our proximity to help our minds work better.

Questions

1) Can you think of a time where you felt overwhelmed or chaotic inside, and you wanted someone to help you through that? What did you want them to do? Were you able to communicate that to them?
2) Can you feel into the benefit of having a grounded person present with you that simply occupies space with you, versus asking questions or trying to help in external ways?

Experiment

Try this activity to get a sense of what it's like to receive the support of another beyond words. Ask someone you trust to sit on the floor with you, back to back. One of you can read these instructions aloud. Find a position that is comfortable, and spend as much time as needed finding it. Once you're there, play with leaning against each other slightly. You can ask each other to sit taller or shift how much weight you add to the posture. When you've settled in, tune into your breathing pattern. Notice it. As you're staying attuned to your breath, see if you can sense the breath of the other person through your backs. Notice how the breath moves in the upper, mid, and lower parts of the back. Do this for two minutes, tracking each other's breathing alongside your own. Notice what happens internally for you: your breathing rate and depth, heart rate, and emotional state. While you are here in this space together, come up with a phrase or word you can use to request this in the future when you need it. No questions asked, just an invitation to center and soothe together.

Over time, learn to ask for what you need. You can say "I don't need any help solving the problem I'm upset about, I just need you to sit with me for a little bit." People in your world want to help you, and need you to teach them how to do that. As you become skilled at doing this, you can start to notice when people are offering support in ways that are not helpful, and translate it to yourself. "Feel" into the support they're offering you, and give yourself permission to let go of the words they're using. You can let them know that their presence with you, caring about you, is the most helpful thing. You can bring to mind (and body) the sensation of feeling the support from the back-to-back experience and give yourself the same level of impact. This is the final level of experience, when you no longer require another person to physically be there for you every time. It's not that you never need someone to be there for you, at all. It's that you have a choice about it. You have options. That is the power of how relationships continue to unfold new, expansive ways of existing for us.

Wow. That makes sense. Even though it doesn't directly fit this situation, one part in particular stuck out to me:

> Some of us are born impacted by those around us in more overwhelming ways than most others. It becomes too risky to reach out for support, because the other person can easily add to our internal chaos without even meaning to. Those of us who feel this way have two options: shrink away and shut ourselves off from others, or learn how to ask for the specific support we are needing to regain balance.

To me, this sums up perfectly why we need to ask for people's help when we feel bad, instead of either lashing out at them or shutting down. Just because we're scared they'll make it worse, or make us angrier, we push them away and retreat into our turtle shells. I wish I had read this Manual a long time ago, and this chapter in particular, especially at the beginning of my journal. Because people who love you don't deserve to have your anger taken out on them, or pushed away.

And if you push people who love you away, you'll never grow.

Even if we don't want to push people away, if you're rude or mean to them they might think you don't want them to help you. When you're sad, or mad, and you need help and support, you have to tell people what you need. You have to ask them to help you or they might not even know you need help. Opening up to people makes you happier.

I try to take these words to heart as I make my way downstairs. It might seem like a small thing, coming down after being so mean to my sweet little sister, but for me it takes effort. I have to be brave.

I walk down the stairs. I have no clue what I'll say to my parents. My sister definitely told them I was mean. And what will I say to my sister? Will she be mad at me?

Everyone's already eating dinner by the time I arrive at the dining room. I'm kind of annoyed and insulted. *Apparently, they just don't really care about you,* that voice that always tries to put you down says. But I know that's not true. They just know I'm stubborn and must have thought that it would be a wasted effort to try to get me downstairs. Especially if I'm "In a Mood," which my parents probably assumed I was because I yelled at my sister. And I guess I was In a Mood. But I'm not anymore. Now I'm just ashamed. And I owe my sister an apology.

"Kylie?" I say tentatively. It took so much work to get that one word out, and now my whole family is staring at me. The room has gone silent.

"What?" she responds defensively.

"I'm -" I choke on the word but I get it out - "sorry."

"It's okay," she says. She can't hold grudges. It makes me smile. But I'm not done. I wouldn't forgive her that easily, and I need to finish apologizing. I need to explain myself.

"I just wanted to finish something, and I overreacted, and I..." I trail off when I realize no one's really listening.

"I said it's okay," she says, smiling. Her curls bob as she laughs. And I realize I don't need a long, heartfelt, scripted apology. Just the fact that I apologized is enough in this case. The fact that she could tell I really meant it was all that mattered.

Instead of coming down surly and silent, I came downstairs openly, and honestly, and that made a big difference in the rest of my family's moods. I know without a doubt that if I had come down grumpy and responded meanly to anyone who tried to talk, my mood would have rubbed off on people, but as is, we're all sitting around the table getting along, talking and laughing. Full of food and full of happiness.

THE EPILOGUE
or, my ramblings about life and happiness

I love those moments when you feel like everything's perfect, that life couldn't be better, and you want to catch the moment in a bubble and stay in it forever. Of course, though, you can't. Life goes on. I used to think that was the sad truth, but after embarking on this journey The Manual sent me on, I don't think that's true anymore. It's not just the good experiences that make life worth living; it's the bad ones too. Because the bad choices you make, and the bad days you have, make life better. Even if it might not feel like it at the time. They give you opportunities to learn about yourself. To grow closer to people. To get stronger and better at feeling the way YOU want to feel. And to be happy with who you are.

My journey hasn't ended. It isn't even close. What's that saying? "Life is a journey, not a destination." If I could push a button and gain all the wisdom I hope I'll gain with age without experiencing the good and bad things I'll see and do, the things I'll learn the hard way, reach my destination without the long journey, would I do it? A year ago, I would have said yes. Now I'm not sure. Because what's the point of life if you don't live it? We need to learn to accept and treasure every moment we're given, even if we don't feel thankful at the time. Because if we don't, we lose the opportunity to grow and change.

And change can be beautiful.

To me, happiness is knowing these truths, being brave enough to confront myself, and knowing that if you have enough strength and determination inside you to seek happiness, it will find you.

I wish you luck on your own lifelong journeys.

~ jamie

COMPREHENSIVE MANUAL FOR
MANAGING INTENSE EMOTIONAL STATES

by Walter M. Cunningham, PsyD

THE BASICS: GET TO KNOW YOUR PROTECTOR BRAIN AND YOUR WISE MIND

The first thing there is to know about managing intense emotional states has to do with the way the human brain works. A gross oversimplification that can be useful here is to imagine two distinct parts of the brain - not a left side and a right side, but a top and a bottom. The evolutionarily newer, top parts of the brain we'll call the Wise Mind, and the older, bottom parts we'll call the Protector Brain. They function in distinctly different ways, which are discussed more thoroughly in the paragraphs that follow.

The most important part of the Wise Mind is called the Pre-Frontal Cortex (PFC for short). This part of the brain develops through the mid-twenties. It manages the human emotional experience; which means children, teens, and anyone without a fully functional PFC often cannot effectively execute emotion-management strategies. Parents and caregivers can direct the attention of the child in the desired pathways of emotion-regulation, with repetition, until the PFC is fully developed. When activated, the Wise Mind helps people make decisions that are good for us, good for those around us, and good for the planet. The Wise Mind is a creative and flexible problem-solver; therefore learning to activate it before approaching challenges is an important first step in the process.

The Protector Brain, as its name implies, has survival in mind. When it perceives threat - whether physical, emotional, or social - it restricts blood flow from the Wise Mind to keep you safe. It shuts down your digestion, and sends you into fight or flight mode. In some situations too big to fight or flee from, the Protector Brain shuts you down, causing you to "play dead." The Protector Brain plays a very important role. When it works appropriately, it is a literal life-saver.

However, the Protector Brain can create some challenges. One challenge is that it sometimes detects and reacts to situations and cues which are not truly threats. While it happens to everyone, people who have experienced some form of trauma often have more frequent and intense "false" alarms. The Protector Brain also cannot shut itself off, but does respond to cues from the body that the environment is safe and free from danger.

The Protector Brain can be over-reactive in people who:
• experience emotions more intensely than others;
• are shy or more inhibited in social situations;
• react quickly with fear or anxiety when others are calm.
The good news is we can learn coping strategies which help them manage the false alarms and function well.

Questions

1) Recall a time recently when you experienced a takeover by the Protector Brain. What thoughts were you having during that time? Was the threat real or perceived?
2) Recall a time your Protector Brain took over and you were able to soothe it and bring the Wise Mind back online. What strategies did you use?

Experiment

Notice when your Protector Brain gets activated. Draw or write about what happens in your body. Ask people you trust to tell you what they notice, too.

THE BASICS PART II: THE BRAIN-BODY INFORMATION HIGHWAY

There is an information highway between the brain in our heads and neurons throughout the body. We have historically believed that changing our emotional state merely required changing a dysfunctional or unhelpful thought. That is certainly true in some cases. However, only a small portion of the communication on that highway is from the skull-brain down into receptor sites in the body. Signals from the body to the brain make up approximately 80% of the massive amounts of information being exchanged on that highway.

What kind of information is being exchanged?

Everything you could possibly imagine, and more. The heart, for example, sends information about heart rate, the variability between beats, blood pressure, and more. The skull-brain takes in this information, interprets it to filter threat and safety, and reacts accordingly. There is also information that comes from the gut and all the muscles in the body (including the face); communicating tension, constriction, restriction, and more for the same purpose: to detect threat.

How can we use this information to create more happiness and health?

First, we must become aware of the signals coming from our body into our brain so they don't take us over. For example, if your stomach gets tight when you think about starting something new, your brain perceives a threat when it is clear the potential threat level is quite low. It may send signals back down to your body to constrict the muscles and prepare to run away.

Once we are able to detect the earliest signals that our brain perceives as threats, we can start to shift the reactionary survival strategy our brains deploy. We can realize that protection isn't needed, yet honor that mechanism within us that seeks safety above all else. We can use specific strategies and tools to shift our internal state from reaction to response.

How do we shift from reaction to response?

The biggest factor is repetition. Once you learn to filter those cues of danger from your body and experiment with the techniques described in this manual, it will take time and repetition to wire up the new pathways in your system. You will no longer immediately believe the thoughts that swirl in your mind; you will learn it is safe to let them settle and begin to make decisions only after the fight, flight, or freeze reaction has passed.

Questions

1) What are the signals your body sends to your brain when you are in each of the three survival reactions of fight, flight, and freeze?
2) Which survival reactions do you experience during intense emotional states such as anxiety/worrying, fear, anger/rage, irritation, and even excitement?
3) What thoughts do you think and actions do you take when your Protector Brain triggers a survival reaction?

Experiment

Have someone trace an outline of your body on a long piece of paper. Choose an emotional state or survival reaction that you'd like to work on gaining more mastery with, and draw how your body's cues feel to you on the paper. There's no right answers - only your answers.

SOOTHING THE PROTECTOR BRAIN

The Protector Brain evolved to be aware of our surroundings. This makes sense when you consider our ancestors, who could be eaten if they didn't pay attention to the environment around them. We can use this tool to our advantage today, when we sense that our Protector Brain has been triggered by strong signals in our bodies. Moving the head and eyes from side to side and up and down activates a reward feedback loop which quiets the alerted lower brain systems.

This is not distraction. When you initiate this process, you are not asking the brain to engage in a thought process about anything in the room. You are merely using the turning head and side-to-side eye movements as a mechanism to soothe the lower brain systems.

Since the Protector Brain receives abundant signals from the body, you'll want to become well versed in its language; the language of **sensation**. This is different from the Wise Mind's assignment of labels on the cumulative experience of sensation and thought; what we call **emotion**. There are two types of feelings then; what we actually physically feel with our bodies (which we can call sensation), and what our minds label that experience. To become a master at shifting your emotional experience, you'll need to develop a focused awareness of your internal experience of sensation. Once you become aware of sensations, you can become aware of uncomfortable sensation and shift it into comfortable sensation. Noticing your surroundings is one way to do just that.

Another tool you can use is training yourself to look for and focus on comfortable sensations within your body. Here's how: when you become aware of uncomfortable thoughts or sensations in the body, look for any place on you that feels comfortable and keep your attention there as long as possible. You can also bring to mind a memory of feeling comfortable, keeping your attention on the memory until you feel it in your body and can focus on the sensation.

Questions

1) What are all of the words you can think of that describe sensation? Think: temperature, movement, texture and shape to get you started.
2) Think about a time you felt incredibly comfortable. Describe it in detail: where were you? who was there? where did you notice the comfort in your body? Notice what sensations are present as you re-visit this memory. Draw them on a body outline if you'd like, or write about it in a journal. Come back to this memory often to build the neural pathway to comfort so you can use it when something uncomfortable starts to creep up.

Experiment

Practice noticing what's around you for the first few times when your Protector Brain is not activated. You're establishing a new neural pathway and strengthening it (like a muscle) so it's much easier to do when you start feeling overwhelmed. Start by scanning your body, from your feet up to your head, and notice any sensations that are present. Rate both your level of discomfort and your level of comfort on separate scales of 1-10 (they won't necessarily add up to equal 10). Notice what's around you, making sure to turn your head at a comfortable pace to look in various directions, and do this several times at a comfortable pace. Assess sensation in your body by scanning feet to head again, and rate the levels of discomfort and comfort again. Note any changes.

PLAY WITH YOUR INTENSE EMOTIONS

It's not uncommon for us humans to adopt our thoughts and feelings as fundamental truths of our core personality or genetic composition. From a scientific and neurobiological standpoint, our thoughts and emotions are essentially the result of neural wiring created by our perception of our experiences. The interplay of our genes and the environment which surrounds us creates the wiring. Genetic influences are being given less and less weight as science is coming to the understanding that genes are not static life sentences, but can and do shift and switch on and off over time in response to experience.

Once we are aware of a pattern of thought or feeling that we have, we can purposefully create experiences that help us shift the old wiring to something more desirable. Try the questions and experiment below in order to create an experience in which you can begin to shift an uncomfortable emotional state.

Questions

1) Think about a situation where you felt overwhelmingly frustrated. Where does that frustration live in your body? What does it physically feel like? Use sensory language from the previous chapter to describe it.
2) What color is associated with that frustration? Don't come up with an answer, simply ask yourself the question and accept the first color that comes to mind. You may actually see the color in your imagination, or the answer might come to you another way. Be open.
3) Now, imagine taking that frustration out of your body and putting it on the chair next to you. What shape is the frustration? Does it have smooth or rough edges; solid lines or fuzzy; and is it moving or does it stay still? How big is it? Describe it in as much detail as possible. Write it down or draw it, using the color you found in the previous section. You may discover new colors as you elaborate on the details.

4) Make that frustration into a character. Is it masculine, or feminine? Does it have facial features? What might it's name be? Perhaps the most important question is: What does it want, and why?
5) What other feelings and thoughts might you like to create characters out of? Worries, fears, anger, rage, sadness, bitterness, even happiness?

Experiment

Now that you have created a frustration character, play with it. You could do this in a number of ways - create a storyline about it, interview it, or draw how it interacts with other feelings and thoughts you have.

MAKE FRIENDS WITH YOUR FEARS

Worries and fears share one thing in common: activation of the Protector Brain. They often represent a belief about physical, emotional, or social safety in our world. The Protector Brain can't distinguish between a perceived threat ("maybe I will feel embarrassed") or a real one (being chased by a tiger), so any threat cues detected by the brain can trip the alarm. As we've previously established, once this occurs, blood flow from the wiser parts of the brain becomes restricted to the survival mechanism. Then we can feel worry, which has physiological components similar to the fight/flight energetic survival strategy, or fear, often associated with the freeze strategy. To create a different neural network for perceived threats, it is important to work with them when you are in a safe, protected space; physically, emotionally, and socially.

Often, our initial response to worry/fear is to push it down, look away, and avoid it as much as possible. This may work temporarily as we become distracted, but without resolution the worry/fear continues to wield power over our mental worlds. When we truly understand this, we can find inspiration to find a safe venue to meet this fear and discover what it's so afraid of. Once we do this, we can use our Wise Minds to think of creative solutions which address the fear and allow us to be in choice about how to move forward.

Questions

1) What are some situations that are real, actual threats? What situations are better classified as perceived (ie, no physical threat to life)?
2) What behaviors, thoughts, and/or sensations clue you in that you are experiencing worry? Does that align with a high-energy state of repetitive thinking, a need to move, or easily-irritated by others?

3) What behaviors, thoughts, and/or sensations clue you in that you are experiencing fear? Do you experience a low-energy state of absent or stuck thinking, a physical inability to move, and desire to either isolate or cling to someone?
4) What people, places, and/or strategies help you feel safe? (Refer back to Soothing the Protector Brain if you get stuck!)

Experiment

The first step is to create safety for yourself. Choose a place that is very comfortable for you. You might like to collect some of your favorite things to look at or touch. Take a few moments to look around, noticing the environment around you. You may ask someone you trust to help you with this, or complete it on your own.

Next, choose the worry or fear you'd like to work with. Imagine it as a character, separate from you. What does it look like? How does it move (or not)? Where is it in relationship to you? What would you name it? Draw or write about it to really help it separate from you. If you become overwhelmed at any point in this experiment, shift your attention back to the place and things that are comfortable to you, and stay there as long as you'd like. When you feel ready, come back to the experiment. You might find that you would like to have someone comforting present with you, and you can ask them to simply be in the room with you or be close to you without asking questions about your experiment yet.

Now, ask the worry or fear what it wants. The first answer you get may not be the best fit - question the worry/fear until you discover what it's trying to protect you from. All worries and fears activate our Protector Brains to protect us from something. What is this worry or fear you've chosen trying to protect you from?

Can you accept the genuine desire of this worry/fear to protect you? Can you see the good place of intention it comes from? Let the worry/fear character know you understand where it's coming from. You can draw this on your paper, write about it, or imagine it in your mind. Tell the worry/fear that your wise self has got this concern under control, so the worry/fear can rest now.

The last step is deciding how to move forward where the worry/fear has ruled your behavior and thoughts. How would you like to handle this situation?

ACCESSING THE WISDOM WITHIN

Built within our nervous/sensory systems exists an internal tuning fork; a directional nudge towards that which is most life-affirming for us. We can learn to tap into this inner resource as an additional authority in our decision-making processes.

Using sensory cues and mental images, you can develop this muscle of inner wisdom. It requires a moment of balance that is void of perceived threats which would activate the Protector Brain. The Wise Mind has connections to the nervous system which allow us to have an awareness of what's arising in our internal landscape, versus the connections of the Protector Brain which merely subject us to its variety of survival reactions.

Sensory cues may come in the form of movement, temperature, sound, texture, and pressure. Some people get sensory information in the form of an image or perception of sound.

Questions

1) Think of situations where you have felt unclear about the best choice to make. What strategies did you employ to look for answers?
2) Have you ever "just known" the right answer or choice for you? How?
3) Read the following words aloud and note the reaction in your body:

NO   NO   NO   NO

NO   NO   NO

4) Now read this set of words aloud and note your internal reaction:

Yes   Yes   Yes   Yes

Yes   Yes!   Yes!

Experiment

Get comfortable in a quiet, emotionally/socially/physically safe place. Quiet your thinking brain (try closing your eyes) and go inside of yourself. Attune to your physical experience as you sit or lie on the floor, chair, or your bed.

Say NO to yourself firmly ten times, as in question 3 above. Identify the sensations, colors, images, shape, and movement your internal experience reacts with. Repeat this process saying YES, noting the sensory reaction you have. You can write or draw these reactions in a journal to help you remember.

Now that you have identified two ends of your tuning fork, test it out. State a very basic, simple truth that is an absolute yes (you can try "my name is _____"). Notice the sensory reaction. Is it a match to the reaction you had for question 4? Now play with something which you feel strongly to be untrue. Note your sensory reaction.

Once you are getting consistent sensory reactions to questions you feel confident are either true or untrue, you can being testing this internal tuning fork in more challenging situations. Remember to always ground yourself in a safe space before attempting to navigate this experiment.

THE IMPACT OF THE INTENSE
EMOTIONAL STATES OF OTHERS

Neuroception is a term coined by Dr. Stephen Porges. It describes a subconscious system for detecting threats and safety. As we have seen, the Protector Brain does not distinguish between an actual life-threatening situation vs. a perceived emotional threat. Our systems have subconscious means of detecting these perceived types of social/emotional threats as a way of keeping us safe from embarrassment, emotional vulnerability, and other emotional deaths.

One example of how it does this is via electromagnetic signal detection. The Institute of HeartMath found that the electromagnetic signal emitted from the heart is detectable up to three feet around it. Heart signals tell us when a person is feeling a negative, threatened state (emotional correlates include frustration or anger), and also when they're feeling a positive, safe, balanced state (emotionally translated as appreciation or gratitude).

Knowing this, we become aware of the impact of others on our own internal state. For example, if you're feeling okay and a person with an agitated state enters your radius of detection, your survival mechanisms react and become activated, creating a type of alarm within you. It makes sense if you think of humans as a herd of sorts. The herd's survival depends on detecting outside threat, and the individual's survival depends on attunement to the herd. It's important to remember that survival activation does not differentiate between physical, emotional, social, nor real vs. perceived threats. A perceived embarrassment in front of peers activates a survival reaction similarly to a lion on the savannah. It's a life-changing realization.

Another empowering piece of information is that our signals impact others, too. When we notice someone in a threatened state, we can intentionally tune into ourselves, create a sense of ease, balance, and gratitude within us, and impact the physiology of the other person. It's a powerful tool when you want to help someone but aren't sure what to say, and for those times you are in disagreement with another and it's going downhill. Often, words alone aren't enough.

Questions
1) Can you recall a time where someone else seemed to impact you on this subconscious level? Maybe they were frustrated or irritated about something else, and you could feel it inside of yourself? Or perhaps you've had the opposite experience, where someone's calm and gentle presence helped you release frustration.
2) How do you experience frustration in your physical body? Remember to use sensory language like color, shape, movement, and texture.
3) How do you experience gratitude in your body?
4) What tools help you get into a state of gratitude, thereby helping you emit positive electromagnetic signals into the space around you?

Experiment

Work through the questions above. Draw or write your answers down and compare. What are the differences? Play with initiating the state of gratitude by bringing to mind a time you felt loved or loving. Imagine the scene as fully as you can, bringing to mind any sounds, sights, scents, and sensations you experienced. Stay there for as long as is comfortable, for at least several minutes. Pay special attention to any sensations you experience around your heart area; perhaps a lightness or warmth that radiates out.

Next, think of a situation you've had feelings of frustration or irritation about. Think about this for a few moments and notice how your body sensations shift. Now let go of that situation and those feelings and turn your attention back to the state of gratitude. See if you can make it as big as it was before. Congratulations - you have demonstrated being able to change your emotional state without anything in your environment shifting!

Now pay attention to your state when you are in close proximity to others. Try to generate a state of gratitude anytime you think of it - for your benefit, and for those around you!

HOW AND WHY IT'S IMPORTANT TO HAVE HEALTHY AND HELPFUL RELATIONSHIPS

The short, simple answer to why it's important to have relationships (whether healthy or not, turns out) is that they help us learn and grow into the best versions of ourselves that can be. If one lives in isolation, they limit the number of ways their brain can expand and take in new possibilities. This expansion of thought and awareness of multiple solutions to problems leads to increased happiness in life. These experiences also widen our window of tolerance, meaning we learn new skills which help us overcome new and varying obstacles.

It's important to have healthy relationships because we learn by experience. If we do not get the parenting that we need to be happy and resilient when we are children, we truly must experience love and support from another person before we can fully know it ourselves and pass it on to others around us. We also develop inner language based on what we hear around us. If we hear "don't be sad, smile" our whole childhood, and never experience another person being okay with our sadness, then we can develop that inner dismissive language ourselves into adulthood. Many parents mean well and simply have never been shown the way to be the parents they truly want to be.

Some of us are born impacted by those around us in more overwhelming ways than most others. It becomes too risky to reach out for support, because the other person can easily add to our internal chaos without meaning to. Those of us who feel this way have two options; shrink away and shut ourselves off from others, or learn how to ask for the specific support we are needing to regain balance. It's of neurological benefit for us to do this; our nervous system is wired to soothe when engaged with non-threatening-feeling others (see the work of Stephen Porges for more detailed information). In other words, we can activate our Wise Minds, think more clearly, and better problem solve our challenges when we activate the relational dynamic in the midst of our internal chaos. It's not about the other person's words or wisdom at all - it's merely the effects of having a calm, grounded person in our proximity to help our minds work better.

Questions

1) Can you think of a time where you felt overwhelmed or chaotic inside, and you wanted someone to help you through that? What did you want them to do? Were you able to communicate that to them?
2) Can you feel into the benefit of having a grounded person present with you that simply occupies space with you, versus asking questions or trying to help in external ways?

Experiment

Try this activity to get a sense of what it's like to receive the support of another beyond words. Ask someone you trust to sit on the floor with you, back to back. One of you can read these instructions aloud. Find a position that is comfortable, and spend as much time as needed finding it. Once you're there, play with leaning against each other slightly. You can ask each other to sit taller or shift how much weight you add to the posture. When you've settled in, tune into your breathing pattern. Notice it. As you're staying attuned to your breath, see if you can sense the breath of the other person through your backs. Notice how the breath moves in the upper, mid, and lower parts of the back. Do this for two minutes, tracking each other's breathing alongside your own. Notice what happens internally for you: your breathing rate and depth, heart rate, and emotional state. While you are here in this space together, come up with a phrase or word you can use to request this in the future when you need it. No questions asked, just an invitation to center and soothe together.

Over time, ask for what you need. You can say "I don't need any help solving the problem I'm upset about, I just need you to sit with me for a little bit". People in your world want to help you, and need you to teach them how to do that. As you become skilled at doing this, you can start to notice when people are offering support in ways that are not helpful, and translate it to yourself. "Feel" into the support they're offering you, and give yourself permission to let go of the words they're using. You can let them know that their presence with you, caring about you, is the most helpful thing. You can bring to mind (and body) the sensation of

feeling the support from the back-to-back experience and give yourself the same level of impact. This is the final level of experience, when you no longer require another person to physically be there for you every time. It's not that you never need someone to be there for you, at all. It's that you have a choice about it. You have options. That is the power of how relationships continue to unfold new, expansive ways of existing for us.

OUR STORY

Jenifer and Brinsley first met in the summer of 2013, on their journeys to understand overwhelming emotions and discover meaningful tools for self-understanding.

We wanted to write this book to give others going through similar challenges a story they can connect to, to feel less alone in their struggles with overwhelming emotions. We're also really excited to share the tools and perspectives neuroscience and mind-body psychology have to offer young teens and their families.

AUTHOR BIOGRAPHIES

Brinsley Hammond-Brouwer lives in Oregon with her parents, younger sister and brother, two cats and an insanely fluffy Goldendoodle. Some things she enjoys are: trees, books, sewing, dance, biking, manatees, blue, Goldendoodles, friends, kittens, drawing, spring, music, Star Wars, robotics, and writing. When she's not reading, she can be found sewing, at the dance studio or volunteering at the library.

Jenifer Trivelli, M.S. resides in the Pacific Northwest and is a mom of two with a graduate degree in Counseling. She specializes in social-emotional education - coaching parents, training organizations, and teaching yoga for kids through her company WiseMind Educational Services LLC. She is the author and illustrator of *Peanut and the BIG Feelings: A Guidebook for Children*.

CPSIA information can be obtained
at www.ICGtesting.com
Printed in the USA
LVHW100104210722
723934LV00006B/309